Someone
Like Me

WORLD BOOK DAY

Quick Reads

We would like to thank our partners in the *Quick Reads* project for all their help and support:

BBC RaW
Department for Education and Skills
Trades Union Congress
The Vital Link
The Reading Agency
National Literacy Trust

Quick Reads would also like to thank the Arts Council England and National Book Tokens for their sponsorship.

We would like to thank the following companies for providing their services free of charge: SX Composing for typesetting all the titles; Icon Reproduction for text reproduction; Norske Skog, Stora Enso, PMS and Iggusend for paper/board supplies; Mackays of Chatham, Cox and Wyman, Bookmarque, White Quill Press, Concise, Norhaven and GGP for the printing.

www.worldbookday.com

Someone
Like Me

Tom Holt

www.orbitbooks.co.uk

ORBIT

First published in Great Britain in March 2006 by Orbit
Reprinted 2006

A CIP catalogue record for this book
is available from the British library.

ISBN-13: 978-1-84149-446-3
ISBN-10: 1-84149-446-1

Typeset by SX Composing DTP, Rayleigh, Essex
Printed and bound in Great Britain

Orbit
An imprint of
Time Warner Book Group UK
Brettenham House
Lancaster Place
London WC2E 7EN

www.orbitbooks.co.uk

For Natalie; may the Hoof
be with you always

CHAPTER ONE

THERE WAS ONE LYING in the road when I got there. She was dead, no need to look up close. You can tell from twenty yards away, when they're lying like that. It always makes me think of an old sack that's been blown away by the wind, or rubbish chucked out in the street. Strange, really. One minute someone's alive, with a mind full of thoughts and memories, and a moment or so later they're just a thing, a skin bag full of meat.

'They've been here, then,' I said.

There was a man who I guess had been waiting for us to arrive. He looked scared, so I knew he'd seen them. You can tell that at a glance, too.

I knelt down beside the dead woman. You know what to look for after a while. She'd been cut about with a blade, but the cuts were all on her wrists and forearms, where she'd been trying to shield her head. Messy wounds, like all cuts, but she'd have lived if that'd been all. What did for her was a long slit, starting just under the navel and going right up to where the collar-bones meet. Just like someone opening a letter. No weapon ever did that.

'How many?' I asked.

'Two,' the man replied.

'Did they get anybody else?'

He nodded. 'In the house,' he said.

That's bad. When they get inside a house full of people, it's like a fox breaking into a hen coop.

'Have you been inside?' I asked. He shook his head. He looked ashamed of himself, but that's stupid. Nobody should have to look at something like that, not unless they're in the trade, like me, and it's their job.

So I went and looked; and I've seen worse. Downstairs there was a boy, about nine years old. Same sort of cuts as the woman had, but his head was missing. That gave me some idea of what I was looking for – a female, most likely, and either old or injured. When they're like that they go for kids because they're easy to pull down. A young, healthy male would go for an adult, so it would only have to kill once, and then it could lie up for a week, maybe even ten days, without having to hunt again.

But the man outside had said there were two of them, so I was probably looking for a nesting pair. My guess was that the female had killed the boy, and the male had gone for the woman out in the street, but since they hadn't dragged the bodies away they must've been startled by something before they had the chance. In that case, there'd probably be another body.

I found him upstairs. He was squatting down in the corner of the bedroom, arms by his side, head forward on his chest. Loss of blood, almost certainly. When I tried to move him, I saw a couple of stab wounds in the chest and gut, and the floor was wet with blood. It had soaked into the old, frayed carpet, which made it squelch underfoot.

The way I saw it, this man had come running in when he heard the kid yelling. Soon as he saw what was going on, he turned and ran up the stairs. He probably tried to barricade himself in, because there was a chair lying on the floor next to him. I suppose he'd been trying to jam the door shut with it. Wasting his

3

time, of course. The door panels were splintered in three places where the female had kicked it or bashed it with her paws. Then she'd got scientific and hacked a big hole in the panel with an axe or one of those wide-bladed hooks they use. After that, all she needed to do was stick her hand through and push the chair away.

He'd had a go at her. I found a sword in the middle of the room, one of those cheap, thin things they sell for home defence. He must've landed at least one on her, because the blade was bent and there was a chunk taken out of the cutting edge. Nobody makes decent steel any more. He couldn't have done her much harm, because there wasn't any blood on the blade. Just enough of a contact to make her angry and scared and all the things you don't want them to be when you're trapped in a room with one of them.

After that, she'd killed him with whatever weapon she was using, but she hadn't stopped to snack. My guess is that she just wanted to get out of there as fast as she could.

I stood there, trying to figure out what to do. At times like that, you've got to keep a clear head. There was just the one of me, and it looked like they'd split up and gone their separate ways after the attack, so I couldn't go after them both. That meant choosing which one to follow.

My first thought was, go for the female. She's killed two people. But then I figured, The female's scared. If I'm right she's weak from old age or carrying some injury. She's not going to want to pick any more fights today. The male, on the other hand, he's killed, but he hasn't had a chance to eat, so he's still hungry. Also, he's probably young and fit, so it stands to reason, he's the one most likely to be a danger.

It wasn't an easy choice to make. None of the choices in this business are easy, I've found.

So I left the dead man and went back downstairs, past the boy, back out into the street. The man I'd talked to earlier was still there, and some other people, neighbours. They all had that blank, stunned look. Most likely it was the first time they'd come so close to an attack.

First thing you've got to do is get people off the street. You won't believe how often it happens that one of them gets chased off or spooked, and an hour or so later it comes straight back and has another go. I guess they realise people are off their guard. So what you have to do is round everybody up and find somewhere secure where they can stay put and wait till we give the all-clear. This time it wasn't a problem. Soon as I explained, they were only too pleased to have someone tell them what to do. There was an old church in the middle of the village, with a tower. I sent them up there, and told them to block the doors with everything they could find.

Next I went back to the attack scene. Didn't take long to find tracks, but they were bloodstained, and I reckoned they must belong to the female, from where she'd been walking on the blood-soaked carpet. The pawmarks went off across the back yard of the house, headed straight for the woods behind the village. Well, I thought, if she's made it to cover, I'm not going in there after her, not without dogs and a lot of back-up.

So that was my choice made for me after all.

I nosed around for maybe a quarter of an hour before I picked up the other one's tracks. It took me a while, but I was able to make a pretty good guess at what it'd done after it killed the woman. Something must've spooked it after it killed her, and it ran off pretty fast up the street till it reached the corner of an old boarded-up shop. It must've stopped there while it caught its breath and calmed down, made sure it wasn't being followed. After that, it carried on down the street a bit until it came to an alley that wound back. There was a pile of old salvaged timber and scrap and stuff, and my guess is that it lay up there while I was in the house.

I was pretty certain it knew there was someone after it by that stage. They always seem to know. An old bloke who'd been in the trade told me they can smell something about the kit we use – saddle-soap or blacking, or the oil we put on our blades to stop them rusting. I don't know if that's true, but it's got to be something of the sort.

I stood by that scrap-pile, and that seemed to be the end of the trail. There weren't any more tracks, or else I couldn't see them, but the bastard thing had to have gone somewhere. Either that, or it was still there.

Another thing the old bloke told me: Never forget to look up.

I saw him. He'd scrambled up to the top of the scrap-heap and flattened himself right down, the way they can when they don't want to be seen. Marvellous, the way they can break up their outline and almost melt away into whatever they're standing on. I'd been right about one thing. It was a young male, maybe four years old, no more than five.

I remember standing there looking at it, and it looking back at me. It was big for its age, a good five-footer. It had on a human coat-of-plates, probably stripped of one of my lot it had killed at some time. Under the coat it had pale brown fur, no markings. For some reason, the picture has stuck in my mind. It was like looking at a cat on a fence, with its back arched, like it's about to spit at you. Every bit of it was tense, which is a sure sign it's about to spring. It had a rusty flat-bladed hook in its right hand, and the claws were out on its left, but as we looked at each other I knew it wasn't going to make a move until I did.

I've heard people say that they're like dogs, they can't actually see you unless you move. I don't believe that. I think they're lazy, like all animals. They don't want to use up their energy

8

unless there's a good reason. My guess is that this one didn't want a fight right then, so it was waiting to see if I'd just back off and go away.

Look, I've been in the trade fifteen years. In that time, you learn a bit about courage. First you learn that when you're close enough to one of them so that you can see the colour of its eyes, nobody's brave. Everybody's scared stiff. The next thing you learn is that nine times out of ten you can beat them if you keep your head – the tenth time is just bad luck, nothing you can do about it. Finding a way of calming yourself down is the only way you're going to make it out alive.

That knack of getting yourself under control is what I call courage, and either you can do it or you can't. It doesn't come with training or practice or experience. It's just there, or it isn't. I can do it, most times, but there's no way of knowing, when you're face to face with one of them, whether or not the knack's going to work today. It's really nothing to do with how dangerous this particular specimen is. I've had no trouble facing up to two-hundredweight seven-year-old males, and I've frozen when I've been facing sleepy old females. Every time, you're starting from scratch, like it's the first one you've ever seen.

This was a time when I froze. Can't begin to say why. Maybe it was because I could see it wasn't going to attack me if I didn't make the first move. Like I knew that this was one time I didn't have to do it just to save my own skin. Or maybe the sight of the dead bodies had got to me more than usual, I don't know. It always gets to you. That's the misery of it.

Anyway, I froze. I looked at it, and it looked at me. How long, I'm not sure. Probably no more than three seconds, but that's a hell of a long time when you're standing there, knowing that there's a good chance you won't be alive thirty seconds from now. I remember all sorts of stupid things about that one: the way the grain of the fur swept back sideways over the cheekbones, the angle the tusks jutted out from the corners of its mouth There are times when in one glance you can see every single hair, every flake of scurf in their coats, every bit of dust and dirt and caked blood matted in the fringe under their chins.

Crazy, the things you notice when you should be thinking about important stuff.

Like I said, no more than three seconds, and then I guess I must've moved, just enough to send it a signal. It jumped, and as it stretched its arms and legs out in the air, suddenly I was someone quite different. I was wide awake, my whole body full of energy. I shifted my weight to my back foot, lifted my shield to cover my left side and watched it come. That's the key. Never take your eyes off them for a split second, or you're screwed. As soon as I felt its weight crashing onto my shield, I pivoted my front foot, giving ground. As I'd hoped, it slid off the shield, lost its balance and fell on the ground. That's when you've got to be quick, because they're so bloody nimble. At best you've got the advantage for two-thirds of a second, and then they're up on their feet again and you're in real trouble.

There wasn't time to get my sword out, so I lifted my left boot and stamped down as hard as I could on its head. Lucky, I caught it right behind the ear, where their skulls are weak. I heard the bone grind and crunch – it's like a thin plank of wood breaking under too much weight. That gave me a full second. I had the sword out nice and quick. I reversed my grip,

11

pressed the point into the hollow just behind the eye-socket, and leaned forward with all my weight.

I remember the first time I did that. You think it's all over, that you've killed it. You look down, and it's stopped moving. Extraordinary feeling, you're alive because it's dead. Almost it's like being reborn. You breathe out, right from the pit of your stomach, and you pull the sword out. And then the bloody thing twitches. They always do. Their heads snap back. Their arms thrash about. Their legs kick out, and you think, Shit, it's still alive. What am I going to do? But it's just a twitch, the muscles relaxing or something like that. All that jerking and kicking doesn't mean anything, except that it really is dead after all.

Then, if you look closely, you can see death coming in its eyes. At first they're wide open, from the panic and the pain. It's straining everything inside, trying to make its body work, but nothing's responding. Then slowly the eyelid starts to slide down. You see life ebbing out of if. You can watch it fade away until there's nothing left except a dead body, garbage, a mess that needs to be cleared away fast in hot weather before it becomes a health risk.

It's a funny thing. In fifteen years. I've killed seven hundred and twenty-six of them. I know that for a fact, because you have to keep a register – regulations or something. Each time, though, that moment takes me completely by surprise. I can never figure out how it works, that process that turns something that moves into something that stays completely still.

13

CHAPTER TWO

WHEN I WAS A KID, my grandad was always going on about how it was before They came here. Of course, he didn't know what he was talking about. He was just telling me what his grandad had told him. Besides, I never listened much, because it sounded like a load of rubbish, stuff you could never believe. According to him, before They came, people used to fly through the air in the stomachs of huge steel birds, and scoot about really fast on the ground inside big steel beetles. Light didn't come from a fire or candles. It sort of trickled down a bit of wire into a little glass bowl hanging from the roof, and you didn't have to mess about with flint and tinder either. It lit itself.

Grandad said that it was just ordinary people like us who built the big cities and the tall buildings, and dug the tunnels where They live now. He said it was safe, back then. You could go anywhere you liked, even at night, with nothing to be afraid of except other people. He said that in those days there was just us and the animals. We'd wiped out all the predators that could harm us, except for a very few in faraway places, and that was why it was possible for the people back then to do all these wonderful things, because there was nothing out there to hunt us. Back then, according to him, it was no big deal for people to live to be sixty.

Well, you know what old people are like. They'll tell you anything, when you're a kid. But since I've been in this job, I've seen a lot of things that made me think about what he said. I've been in the tunnels, for one thing, and I'm damned sure They didn't dig them. I've gone out as far as the old town, where it's all overgrown and fallen down, and I've found bits of machines in the bramble-fuzz, or sticking up out of the dirt. I'm not saying I believe half of what Grandad told me, even now. All the same, it makes you think. For instance if what they tell us is true, and it was giants who built all the buildings and houses, how come the doors are our size, and not twelve feet high?

15

Not that it matters a damn, because that was then and this is now, and even Grandad never had anything to say about where They came from, or why. They just appeared, he said, one day, out of nowhere, and by the time people had realised what was happening and were prepared to believe it, it was too late. Grandad told me once that a million people used to live in this town. How he got hold of that number I have no idea. Nowadays I don't suppose there's a million people in the whole world.

So, I was telling you about how I killed the young male.

After I was sure it was dead, I was in two minds. I said to myself, I've done the job. I've got away with it in one piece. Only a bloody fool pushes his luck. But then I started thinking that there wasn't just one of them but two, and the one that had killed twice was still on the loose somewhere, and – well, this sounds stupid but it's how you think – it was still early in the day, too early to pack up work and go home. Then I got to thinking, I can find the female. I've got a clear trail to follow. If I'm right and she's old or feeble, she'll come back here where she knows there's easy pickings. If I let her go this time and she comes back, I'll have this whole job to do again, and next time the trail might not be so clear, or it could be raining, or I could have a headache.

There's all kinds of little things like that. They don't make much of a difference, but sometimes a little is all it takes. I've known good men in this trade who've died because of a pulled muscle, or a cold, even. When there's one of them coming at you and you've got half a second or less to decide what to do, anything that slows you up or hinders you is enough to kill you. Do it now, I thought to myself. Today while you're still fresh.

Maybe it was because I'd seen what it'd done to the man in the house, or the kid. Probably not. Another thing you can never afford to do is get angry with Them. They're stronger and faster than we are, They can hide better and creep up more quietly. We can only hunt them down and kill them because we're smarter than them, and getting angry makes you stupid.

Anyway, I went back round the side of the house and picked up the female's trail. Easy, like I said just now, because she'd trodden in blood after she killed the man. Just as I'd thought, she was heading out to the woods, up above the village.

Now, normally I wouldn't be stupid enough to follow one of them into dense cover, like a wood. But I knew that area pretty well, and I had an idea she wasn't headed back into the forest. There's a bit of a dip halfway between the village and the edge of the wood, and if you know where to look, you can find an entrance to the tunnels. It was all buildings there a long time ago, but there'd been a fire at some point. Then the brambles and the heather grew up where the ground was sweetened with the ash. I was prepared to bet she lived in the tunnel. It's their nature, you see. They grow up underground in the dark. It's where they feel at home.

So I made a sort of deal with myself. If it turned out she was headed for the woods after all, I'd give up and go home. If she'd gone down the tunnel, then I'd give it a try. It sounds a bit daft, but I'm happier down a tunnel than in the woods. It's what I'm used to, after fifteen years hunting them. Down a tunnel, in the dark, I know the rules.

I like it when I'm right about something, but it can be a pain in the bum at times. Just as I'd been expecting, the tracks led me straight to that dip I was telling you about. I followed them right up to the tumbledown old building where the tunnel mouth was.

That's when I should've stopped and used my head. Really, you see, it was a two-man job. One man with the lantern, the other with a short spear or a crossbow. If I was going to do it on my own, I couldn't have a light – no spare hand to hold it with, see. But that didn't bother me particularly. I've done some good work in the dark, though I say so myself. I've got good ears, and I can smell Them almost as well as They can smell us. What you need for tunnel work is good hearing, patience, a cool head and a short, sharp knife. Well, at any rate, I had the knife.

You do some daft things in this business.

So I got down on my hands and knees, and nosed about in the brambles like a dog till I found the entrance. Not hard to spot, actually. My guess is, once upon a time it was a proper doorway, an arch, plenty high enough to walk through without lowering your head. But as the years went by it got all clogged up with fallen leaves, and they rot down into soil, and so the arch got buried. Then stuff started growing in the sweet soil there, brambles and withies and that sort of thing. And it's got to the point now that you need to turn round and crawl in backwards just to force a way in without getting your face all scratched up.

Before I started to crawl, I took the knife out and tucked it up my left sleeve, good and handy when I needed it. I thought about taking the sword, but down in the tunnels there just isn't room to swing something like that. So I unbuckled the belt and stuck it under a tangle of brambles, out of sight. You can get the sack for leaving your kit lying about, which strikes me as a bit harsh.

Once I was in through the curtain of tangled stuff, I stopped and listened, but all I could hear was my own breathing. It's important when you're down the tunnels to take it nice and slow and easy, because if you get out of breath you can't hear anything over the racket of your own puffing and panting. I took a long, deep sniff, too, but I couldn't make anything out other than the usual smells you get in tunnel mouths. Earth, rotten leaves, damp, stale air, and the filthy shitty smell that hangs about in those places, don't ask me why. I was a bit surprised that I couldn't smell blood, since I knew it'd trodden in the stuff earlier. But I remembered an old-timer telling me that if They get blood on their feet, They'll stop and lick it off just to keep from giving Themselves away. Smart.

Once I was ten yards or so inside the tunnel it was pitch-dark, so I couldn't see a damn thing. But I could feel something smooth and hard under the palms of my hands as I crawled along, rather than damp earth, so I risked it and stood up slowly. That far down, the wind can't blow in leaves and stuff, so the tunnel's not all blocked up and you can stand upright. I knew from other tunnels I'd been in when I had a lamp with me that the smooth hard stuff I could feel was most likely tiles. That's what the people who built the things used to cover the walls and the floors with.

Amazing, really. There must be thousands of tiles for every ten yards – that's millions all told. Imagine what the tunnel-builders must've been like, to be able to make and lay a couple of million tiles. These days, there's nothing people make that you can count in the millions – not arrowheads or nails or anything. They must've had thousands of people back then who did nothing all day but make tiles, just so the floors of these tunnels could be kept dry.

The drill is, you walk along as quietly as you can, keeping your ears and nose open all the time, and you count how many steps you take. Every thirty steps is my rule. Every thirty steps I stop, listen for a count of ten, and take five great big deep breaths, nice and slow. You've got to have a pattern when you're down there, because otherwise it's so fatally easy to lose track of what you're doing or where you are. I heard a story once about one of our lot who was blind, couldn't see at all even in broad daylight. But he'd found and killed more of Them than anybody else in his squad, because down in the tunnels seeing doesn't help you at all, but a blind man's so used to going by what his other senses tell him that really, he's in his element. Anyhow, I kept going, counting my footsteps. Stop, listen, sniff – bit like a dog, I guess, when you take it somewhere it's never been before.

Anyhow, there was nothing to hear, and nothing to smell, so either it'd never come that way after all, or else I wasn't trying hard enough, and I was missing all the signs.

I kept on moving. I was doing what I

generally do when it's not going how I'd expected. I was promising myself. Another thirty steps and if I still haven't heard anything, I'll turn back. Then, thirty steps later, I made myself the same promise, and so on.

The idea is, of course, to keep yourself from panicking, which isn't so easy to do, even if you've done it all before more times than you like to think about. Somehow, it's easier to keep going if you can tell yourself you've got somebody's permission to run away, even if it's only permission from yourself.

I'd more or less decided to pack it in and get out of there when I smelt something. It wasn't anything I'd been expecting – not blood, or the stink of Their sweat, or that very slight freshness in the air that tells you you're close to a junction with another tunnel or a vent shaft. Looking back, I think the reason I managed to keep going was that I didn't recognise the smell. It was one of those kitchen smells you remember from when you were a kid, herbs and spices and stuff. I'm no expert, but I think it was rosemary. Whatever it was, I couldn't begin to imagine what it was doing down a tunnel where They came and went. So I closed my eyes

– you feel better in the dark with your eyes closed, don't ask me why – and pressed on.

Wasn't long before I found out where the smell was coming from. I tripped over it, literally. That's a bad thing to do in the tunnels, because you can't help making a hell of a racket. First there's your boot bashing into whatever it is you're tripping over. Then your bootsoles scuff as you try and keep your balance, then a thud as your shoulder hits the tunnel wall. It's a bit like lighting a fire on a hilltop in the dark. Suddenly, everything within a square mile knows exactly where you are.

I lurched into the wall and slid down against the smooth tiles. Funny thing is, I'd guessed what it was as soon as my foot caught in it. In the dark, you get the knack of recognising the feel of things, and I knew straight away that my boot had hit bone. It's nothing at all like stone, a bit like old, dry wood but denser. Also, as I connected with it, there was another whiff of that herb smell.

I found myself sitting on the tunnel floor, and I reached out to touch the thing I'd tripped over. First thing I felt was cloth – quite thin and fine, very smooth, maybe silk or something like that, which is the kind of thing women wear rather than men. Next, my fingers touched bone. There's no mistaking how it feels under your fingertips, dry and slightly rough. It was quite big and rounded, and after a bit my fingers slid into holes that were plenty big enough to be eye-sockets. A skull, then – somebody's skull.

I carried on until I'd found the neck-bone, and I followed that down to a pair of collar-bones. The rosemary smell was quite strong, but there wasn't any stink of bone or rotten flesh. That told me that the bones had been down there a very long time, long enough for the ants to have stripped off every last scrap of meat and skin. I guess they didn't like the taste of the silk, so they'd left it alone.

Over the silk I felt ordinary cloth, probably linen. I found a pocket, and in it some very dry bits of stick or twig. I took a pinch of them between finger and thumb and held them close to my nose. That was where the rosemary smell had been coming from. Herbs. My guess was that the ordinary-feeling cloth was an apron. A woman, then, most likely. She'd been cooking in her kitchen, with some rosemary leaves in her pocket. Probably she'd just gathered them fresh off the bush that morning.

I really wanted to go back then, but I couldn't make myself do it, not with her lying there next to me. I knew a man once who had this bad dream. He had it over and over again, four or five nights in a row and then it'd go away again and he'd be all right for a bit until it came back and the whole thing started off again. In his dream, he'd be waking up in bed in the morning. He'd turn round to give his wife a kiss, and she'd be there lying next to him but she was dead, all shrivelled up into a skeleton, with the skin stretched tight over her skull and her hair spread out on the pillow all round her. He'd jump up, in his dream, and run next door to the kids' room, and they'd be the same, lying in bed, just bones and withered skin, like thin rawhide.

Sometimes he woke up then, other times he'd dream he ran out into the street, and there were more of them, dead people sitting up against the walls of houses, all shrivelled away. He told me that when he woke up after the dream, he was always blazing angry, as though it was somehow all his fault, but he wanted to blame someone else and take it out on them.

Well, I was feeling angry as I sat there next to the dead woman. Odd thing is, I wasn't really angry with Them for killing her. It was more like I was furious with myself, but I couldn't figure out what it was I'd done wrong. All I could think of was how stupid it'd be if They found me there in the dark and killed me all because I'd tripped over some old bones. Like it was the woman's fault, for leaving her dead body lying about where peopie could fall over it. Crazy, but you catch yourself thinking all sorts of weird shit in the dark.

I made an effort and pulled myself together. If there were any of Them about, it was a pretty safe bet They'd heard me. Question was, would They scamper away and hide, or would They come after me? It could be either, depending on how many there were, whether They were scared or hungry, whatever. I remember thinking, do They have to play games and tricks on Themselves to make them keep going when they're frightened? Are They hunting me yet, or am I still hunting Them?

Whichever way it was, I knew for sure I wasn't doing myself any favours hanging about there. Chances were, if They'd been using this tunnel for any length of time, They'd know about the skeleton and They'd have a pretty good idea where it was. In fact, They could use it as a sort of alarm, to let them know if anyone was coming. It struck me as a bit hard that once They'd killed the poor woman, They could use her body against me like that.

Well, these things work both ways.

I had to be very careful, so as not to make any noise. I got down on my knees and felt carefully till I'd found her ribcage. I got a good firm grip on her and lifted her up, just enough so her bones wouldn't trail on the floor and make a noise. Then I started forward, carrying her in my arms.

She didn't weigh hardly anything. Bones don't. They're very light once all the muscle and marrow and stuff have gone. Even so, it was hard going, let me tell you, because of having to keep dead quiet all the time. I couldn't put her down to rest my arms for fear of making a racket or one of the bones dropping off, so I had to keep moving. If the idea I'd had was going to be worth the effort, I had to go at least fifty yards, more if possible.

In the end I think it was more like seventy.

Anyhow, when I simply couldn't go a step further, I laid her down, gently as I could, and shuffled back a few feet to wait and see what happened.

Simple enough idea. If They knew where she was, fine. What They wouldn't be expecting would be for her to have moved seventy-odd yards up the tunnel. With any luck, if They were coming for me, They'd come blundering along not expecting to meet with anything, trip over her and come crashing down right where I'd be waiting.

So I didn't exactly feel wonderful about it, using a poor dead woman as a trap, like she was just a *thing*. I couldn't help thinking. That's what They've been doing. On the other hand, I reckoned that whoever she was, she wouldn't mind helping a fellow human in a bad place – sort of her way of getting even with them for killing her.

I can't say I worried too much about it, at that. I think I'm a very different person when I'm down a tunnel in the dark. At least, I hope so.

CHAPTER THREE

YOU'VE GOT TO BE patient in this line of work. If you can't stay still and quiet, you won't last long. The trick is, like with any sort of hunting. You've got to learn to think like They do. Like, if I was one of Them and I heard a noise, how long would I wait and listen before I set off to do something about it? The problem is, of course, They don't think like us, and we haven't got a clue how They do think, because They're so different. You've got to try and learn, by watching Them, remembering all you can.

So I sat there in the tunnel, behind my pile of bones, and I waited. To begin with, I had the fidgets pretty bad. It happens sometimes. You feel like you can't bear to keep still a moment longer, but you do, somehow. But it wears off, and after that you've got to be very careful you don't let your mind wander. Easily done. You can even fall asleep. Anyway, it's bloody hard keeping track of time, so I can't honestly tell you how long I'd been waiting when one of Them turned up.

Bloody hell, didn't it make me jump. I guess it was because I'd been down there so long in the dead silence. Thinking back, of course, it can't have been any louder than the row I made when I fell over exactly the same pile of bones, but to me it sounded like a roof falling in. For a split second. I forgot where I was, what I was doing, what was going on, all that. Then I remembered, and I started groping for my knife.

You do stupid things when you're all wound up. I knew for a fact I'd put the knife up the sleeve of my shirt, so it'd be handy when I needed it. I knew that perfectly well, but even so the first thing I did when I heard the racket was reach down to my belt. That's where the knife-sheath usually is. Pure instinct, see. As a result, I wasted two seconds, maybe even three, before I managed to get my hand on the knife and pull it out. That's a very long time, three seconds.

Meanwhile, it must've fallen flat on its face over the skeleton, because I heard a crack, one of the poor dead woman's ribs breaking. Then I could hear claws scrabbling on the tiles as it tried to get up. I guess claws are a handicap on a smooth surface. By now my brain was working again – in situations like that, you'd be surprised how fast you can think – and I leaned back from the waist to put as much distance between me and it as I could manage.

Distance means time, you see. I needed time to figure out exactly where it was, because I couldn't see to stab it, I had to calculate where to stick the knife by what I'd heard and what I could remember. In the end I made a guess. I reached forward and jabbed. I felt the knife go into something, a good two inches, and then stop. That meant I'd hit bone. I gave the knife a hard twist to free it – if you're not careful They twist and thrash around when you stick Them, and that can jerk the knife out of your hand – and pulled it back.

Something hit me in the face. Looking back, I think it was probably a foot, kicking out wildly in pain. It caught me on the side of the jaw. My head went back and met the tunnel wall. That was bad, because there wasn't anywhere further for it to go. I was caught between the kick and the wall like a bit of steel between the hammer and the anvil. I remember doing a sort of check, to see if my jaw was busted or just bruised, then it was back to business. I kicked out with both feet, and I connected with something firm. Muscle – I'm guessing either leg or shoulder. I must've pushed it away from me a bit, because the next thing I knew was something sharp scratching across my face – just the claws this time, rather than the whole foot. I slashed with the knife at where I guessed the leg ought to be, but I missed, and something dug hard into the pit of my stomach.

All in all, I wasn't doing as well as I'd hoped, I'd landed one good stab on the bastard, but it didn't seem to be slowing it down so you'd notice. Meanwhile it had given me a bash in the face and knocked all the wind out of me, and I'd lost my element of surprise. I was running out of time, I knew that, so I grabbed with my left hand and caught hold of what must've been its shoulder. Before I could stab again, though, it wriggled free and I could hear it scampering up the tunnel. I couldn't follow, because the bones were in the way.

I sat down and caught my breath. No point in trying to follow. Very dangerous, too, if it

33

turned round suddenly while I was chasing flat-out after it. Instead, I made myself breathe slowly, till my pulse was back to normal. I tried to think things through. I'd stabbed it. That meant there'd be the smell of blood, I could follow that. Also, there'd probably be blood spilt on the tiles, which I'd be able to feel. Chances were, now that it'd been cut about a bit, it'd be more interested in getting away than coming after me, so the choice to go on or turn back was mine to make. If I went on after it, it'd be me hunting it, rather than just self-preservation. That didn't necessarily mean it'd be less dangerous, of course – far from it. They're like people in that respect. Pain and fear make them cunning and vicious.

I thought it over, and I said to myself, Well, you've come this far. And if you don't finish it today, chances are you'll have to do it all over again from scratch another day. Then it struck me that I'd been assuming there was just the one of them down here. If there were two, or more, even, I could still find myself in a whole lot of trouble if I carried on. Still, I thought, if you start thinking like that you'll never get anything done.

It was more important than ever now to make no noise. It was tricky getting over the skeleton, because obviously it had been moved when my enemy fell over it. So I took the time to feel my way, stretching out my arm until I found it with the tips of my fingers. After that I could get past the bones without treading on anything, and I started looking for spilt blood. It wasn't hard to find. In fact, I nearly slid on it. That told me I'd stabbed the bugger deep enough to make it bleed a lot, and nothing slows an animal up like loss of blood.

I knew that because it'd happened to me once. In a wood rather than a tunnel, but I can remember just what it was like. I'd been badly cut and I was leaking blood all over the place. First I felt tired, then sort of lightheaded, like I'd had a drink or two. I started to think that it really didn't matter too much if They caught me and killed me, just so long as I could stop making the effort of dragging myself along. All I wanted to do was sit down and rest. Staying alive just wasn't that big a deal any more.

I thought about that, and I reckoned the sensible thing would be to keep going on slow and steady, give it time to bleed a bit, until it got tired and slowed down. I'd have no trouble following it, after all, and the longer it ran, the weaker it'd get. Sooner or later its strength would give out, and then I could finish it off nice and easy.

So I took my time, stopping every few yards to stoop down and poke about with my fingers till I found a wet patch on the floor. Not that I really needed to do that, because I could smell the blood easily enough. It's not a smell you can mistake for anything else, a cross between honey and iron filings. I remember thinking, That's the hard bit out of the way. All I've got to do now is stay calm and patient, and it's in the bag.

Of course, that's a bloody stupid attitude, and I was lucky to get off as lightly as I did.

Probably what saved me was going along slow and steady. If I'd been hurrying, I most likely wouldn't have noticed the slight change in the air until it was too late. As it was, I remember thinking, the air feels a bit cooler here, and I was just about to stop when it jumped me.

I think I mentioned already, cooler air generally means a junction, where a side-tunnel branches off the main run. What it'd done, of course, was squat down in the mouth of the side-tunnel to wait for me. Because I was walking more slowly than it was expecting, it jumped out a little bit too early. Instead of landing on my back and pulling me down under it, all it managed to do was push me sideways into the wall. Naturally I had my knife out ready, and as soon as I realised what was going on, I lashed out. But the knife didn't slide in easily like it'd done the first time. It hit something hard – armour, most likely – and glanced off, and that pulled it right out of my hand. I heard it clatter on the ground, and that was a very bad feeling, I can tell you.

At least I managed to keep my head. As soon as I'd figured out that it had messed up, I took a long stride forward, to get out of the way, and turned round sharply. I only had a vague idea of where it was likely to be, but I was fairly certain I was out of reach till it moved forward. I was listening like mad, trying to pick up on its breathing or the sound of its claws on the tiles, but I couldn't hear anything. That told me it was standing still, probably listening for me same as I was listening for it.

I was also trying to figure out where my knife was likely to have landed. That was pretty bloody important. I couldn't very well get down on my hands and knees and scrabble about till I found it, but without it I didn't stand a chance. What I really wanted to know was whether it had a weapon of any kind, or just its claws and teeth. It's a crazy business, fighting right up close against something you can't even see.

Now there comes a time in a fight like this one where you find yourself thinking, Sod this, let's just get it over and done with, one way or the other. It's a calculated risk. If you give it a go and you get it wrong, you're screwed. On the other hand, standing still and waiting for something to happen isn't the safest thing in the world, either. Then it suddenly struck me: the side-tunnel.

Because I hadn't heard it move, I was fairly sure it was stood there, trying to hear me breathe so it could get a fix on where I was. If I was right, that meant it hadn't moved much from where it landed after jumping out at me. In that case, it'd still be more or less opposite the junction.

I could use that. If I felt my way nice and

quiet over to the opposite wall, then followed that into the mouth of the junction and kept going, it stood to reason I could go round the bugger and come up behind it without it knowing. If I could do that and maybe get my hands round its throat, or my boot in its kidneys, maybe I wouldn't need the knife after all. I could either strangle it or stun it long enough to find the knife and cut its throat.

Had to be worth a try, I thought. If it heard me, of course, most likely it'd try and jump me again, but I'd be expecting that, I could be ready. In any case, it had to be better than standing still.

Moving quietly is all about doing things a little bit at a time. You need to break down every movement into little pieces. You don't just take a step. First, you lift your heel off the ground. Then you stop and check your balance. Then you can lift your whole foot, and after that you do the same in reverse – toe down first, stop, check, then the heel goes down and you carefully shift your weight.

It takes some getting used to. You're having to figure out every detail of something you'd usually do without thinking about it at all. The only way you can do it is by taking your time. Everything slows down except your brain. It feels like a week between lifting your foot and putting it down again, and mostly what you're thinking about is breathing. It's no good holding your breath, because you're almost certain to make a noise when you finally let the breath go. Instead you've got to breathe in real slow, hold it just a second or so, then breathe out again, slow as you like, and keep it going like that, all the time. That takes real concentration. You just don't have the brainpower to think about anything else while you're doing it.

Strange, really, how something completely ordinary like taking a breath can suddenly turn into the most important thing in the world. I guess you could call it paying attention to detail, but I think it goes further than that. I think that when things get really tight, you need to concentrate on the really basic stuff. If you can get that right, everything else ought to follow.

Sometimes, though, you can do everything pretty well perfect, and you still screw up. The stupid thing was, it was having my dearest wish come true that nearly did for me. I found my knife. Trouble was, I found it by stepping on it, and that made a noise.

As soon as I heard it scrape on the tiles under my foot, I knew what had happened. That was when things started coming at me fast.

I heard it grunt. It probably didn't mean to. It was the effort of making a spring, I suppose, and maybe leaping out at me hurt, because of where I'd wounded it. Anyhow, I heard it and my instinct was, duck, get down out of the way, and as I was doing that, I remember thinking, Well, if I'm going down, I might as well pick up my knife along the way.

It landed on me while I was bent forward, and for a split second I was sure the shock must've broken my spine. I was pushed down, my knees folded, and I can still remember how much it hurt when my chin hit the hard floor, with its weight as well as mine pressing down on me. I felt my teeth come together with a hell of a crack – lucky I didn't bite my tongue in half – but the good thing was that even as I went down, my fingertips touched the knife handle. That was a good moment, like meeting an old friend you thought you weren't ever going to see again.

41

I wriggled my fingers about until I'd got a firm grip. Problem was, of course, that the hand with the knife in it was trapped under me, and I was trapped under the bastard thing that was attacking me.

That was when it bit me.

All those years I'd been in the trade, and I'd never been bitten by one of Them before. What got to me was the sheer pain of it. It's not like being stabbed or cut, or even like breaking a bone. To give you some idea, imagine what it's like when someone pinches you with their fingernails, and then think of how bloody strong those jaws of Theirs are. I've seen one of Them hanging off a man's arm with both its feet off the ground, like a terrier hanging off a bit of rope by its teeth. I've seen Them tear off hands and feet with a shrug of Their heads. No wonder They can bite.

This one had got its teeth into my left shoulder, right on the round bit of muscle at the top. It's a wonder it didn't just bite it clean off. I remember thinking, Well, that's my left arm buggered up for good: I was pretty calm about it, because when things are happening really fast, somehow there isn't time to panic.

You realise something, and accept it.

At the same time, of course, there was the pain. I wanted to scream, but I couldn't. In fact, it was like the scream was welling up inside me, and if I couldn't get it out I was going to burst open. But I opened my mouth and no sound came out, and I realised it was because I didn't have breath left to scream with.

That was a pretty bad moment, and I reckon that I was not too far off being done for. Looking back, I mean. At the time, there was just the pain, and another part of me that was separate, like it was in another room watching through a window and saying, Oh well, too bad.

Thinking back, I can work out more or less what happened. It bit into my shoulder and pulled back, trying to tear off the chunk of meat it had in its mouth. That was what saved me, believe it or not. As it pulled back, it took some of the weight off my arm, the one I was holding on to the knife with.

Quite suddenly I realised I could move that arm. I tugged on it – I felt a nasty stabbing pain in the tendon just behind the elbow, but that was the least of my problems – and quite unexpectedly it came free, still holding the knife. Without stopping to think, I reached behind me and stuck the knife in, hoping I'd connect with something.

I connected all right. I felt the knife slide in, and as it did so the bastard's jaws tightened in my shoulder, and the pain made me dizzy for a second. That was when I got a stroke of luck. It was still trying to pull away, and as I twisted the knife to get it free, it jerked violently – pure reflex, I guess, like the way your knee flexes if you bang your kneecap on something – and shifted its weight over to the right.

That really hurt my shoulder, and without realising what I was doing I kicked out with both legs. All I kicked was the floor, but hard enough to upset the bastard thing's balance. It slid half off me and hung by its teeth in my shoulder, so that all its weight came down on my hand and the knife it was holding, driving the blade much deeper into the wound than I could ever have managed to do.

It squealed and jackknifed, each movement banging the knife-hilt hard on the tiled floor. I felt its grip loosen in my shoulder, and I saw I had a chance. Letting go of the knife, I put my right hand on the ground, palm flat, and pushed with all the strength I had left. My enemy was still thrashing and bucking forwards and backwards on the ground, I pushed hard with both feet and my one good hand, and it slid off my back onto the floor.

A voice inside my head was saying, Go on, stab it now, while you've got the chance, and I knew that was what I had to do. Finish the bloody thing off, before it got away or turned on me again and killed me.

But I didn't, and even now, years later, I'm not sure why. It'd have been different, I know, if I'd managed to keep hold of the knife. But I hadn't, so in order to kill it, I'd have had to grab hold of it and try and keep it still with one hand while I felt and prodded about for the knife with the other. And I didn't want to do that, for some reason. I couldn't see it, naturally, but I could hear it slapping and banging as it twisted and squirmed about on the floor, and – well, I guess the only word for it is squeamish. I didn't want to touch the disgusting thing again. I just wanted it to die as soon as possible, so I could go home.

God, that sounds so stupid. After all, I'd been

wrestling with it, I'd had its claws digging in me, it'd bitten my shoulder half off, and I'd knifed it twice. Touching it – well, surely I was way past that. But that's what stopped me. It was a bit like when you're a kid and there's a dirty great big spider crawling across your pillow. You know, in your mind, that you're about a hundred times bigger and stronger than it, but you still lie there frozen solid, yelling for Daddy to come and rescue you, rather than balling your fist and just squashing the bugger.

It's not fear, see, it's disgust. Somewhere deep down, you believe that if you touch it, it'll make you dirty, so you can't make yourself do it, no matter how hard you try. That's how I felt right then, with it writhing around on the floor a few inches away from me, and my knife stuck inside it. Besides, I was absolutely sure it was going to die in just a few seconds, and then—

But it didn't. It just carried on and on with the bumping and flapping around, until at last I couldn't take it any more. I got to my knees and crept forward towards it, and that was the stupid thing. Something bony and very, very hard hit me in the face, and I went out like a snuffed candle.

CHAPTER FOUR

I OPENED MY EYES and it was still dark. For a
second I was really scared, until I remembered
about being down a tunnel, and the fight. That
explained why my shoulder was hurting so bad,
and why there was such a strong smell of sweat
and blood. Then I remembered how I'd left
matters.

I groped about on the floor for a bit, hoping
it had died while I was out cold and I'd find its
body, but all I could feel was a few sticky pools.
That told me I'd been out long enough for the
blood to begin drying. It also meant that I
hadn't killed it. It'd been well enough to get
away, taking my knife with it.

That changed a whole lot of things. It meant
I'd failed, of course. Also, I'd got myself pretty
badly carved up, and nothing to show for it.
Back then, the Pest Control Board was much
fussier about proof. If you wanted to claim the

47

bounty on a kill, you had to have something to show them – the head, for choice, or if that wasn't possible and you had a good excuse, you could get away with an arm or a scalp, something they could nail up and show the ratepayers they were getting value for money.

Now my guess was that I'd stuck it well enough that it'd die of something or other soon enough, if only loss of blood. But I couldn't take that to the Board offices and get paid for it. I tried moving my left arm, but all I got was pain. That was it, then. Chances were that the arm would have to be amputated, and even if it wasn't, that was the end of my career in the trade. I felt angry about that, and really stupid. I thought, it'd have been better if the bastard thing had killed me. What use is a one-armed man to anybody? Might as well be dead as crippled with no money.

Well, I didn't get over that exactly, but I managed to cram it away in the back of my mind, mainly by thinking about the really bad mess I was in. Down a tunnel, badly chewed up, no weapon, and who was to say there weren't half a dozen of Them down there with me? Suppose the one I'd been fighting had crawled away to where the rest of fhem lived, told them about me and where it had left me, and They were on Their way right now to finish me off.

Then I thought, Don't be stupid, They don't talk to each other like people do, They're animals. Even so, I was fairly certain They'd be able to smell my blood. I had to get out of there as quickly as possible, number one priority.

Then I remembered, I'd fought the bastard at the junction of two tunnels, and now I'd lost my bearings. It'd have been all right if it hadn't knocked me out, but waking up like that had screwed my sense of direction. I felt about on the floor and found the walls, but I couldn't figure out which was the way I'd come by and which was the side-tunnel. I hadn't got a clue where I was, or which tunnel was the way out.

That was pretty bad, but at least it cleared one thing up for me. I stopped wishing it had killed me and I was dead. I realised I really wanted to stay alive, even with a useless left arm. Being scared helps with issues like that, trust me.

All very well saying to myself, It's all right, I've decided I won't die after all. I'd made the choice, but I had a very bad feeling that it wasn't going to be up to me. Even if there

weren't any more of Them, and the one I'd
been fighting had leaked out all its blood and
died curled up in a corner somewhere, that still
left me lost in the dark in the tunnels, no clue
which way to go. And of course I'd lost a fair bit
of blood myself by this point. It'd be easy as pie
to go the wrong way, end up deep inside the
maze, pass out from exhaustion and blood loss,
and wake up to find I'd died. That'd be a really
stupid way to waste the only life I'd ever have.

Sometimes when something like that hits
you, you panic. Other times, it cools you right
down and makes you start thinking. I'd like to
pretend I'm the sort of man who pulls himself
together and copes with a crisis, but I know it
doesn't work like that. It all depends on a whole
load of things, and it's too complicated to
explain or understand. Anyhow, I got my head
together and tried to think my way out.

Stood to reason, I told myself. The tunnel I
came up by was the tunnel that had blood in it
– the blood it had leaked from the first wound,
which I'd followed while I was tracking it. So I
waddled about on my hands and knees for a bit,
sniffing like a dog, and I found the blood trail.
That was easy. Problem was, it ran two ways.

That puzzled me for a bit, until I realised that one of the trails was from the blood it had slopped everywhere as it ran off, after I'd been knocked out. I couldn't tell just by the smell and the feel which trail was the older one, so I was screwed. One trail led back to the light, safety, staying alive, going home. The other would lead me after my wounded enemy, further into the darkness, to where its mates might well be waiting for me.

To make matters worse, when I scouted round a bit more, I found out that there was a blood trail leading down the third tunnel. That really fazed me, till I figured out that it must've run down one tunnel, stopped, come back and gone off down another. What it meant in practice was that instead of a fifty-fifty chance of guessing the right direction, I was down to one in three. Fucking marvellous.

Well, in a situation like that, what do you do? It's like there's an audience you can't see sat watching you, stuffing their fists in their mouths so you can't hear them laughing. In other words, this time I panicked. I couldn't have moved even if I wanted to. I sat with my back to a wall, knees drawn up under my chin, my useless left arm just flopped by my side – I could feel my knuckles on the cold tiles, but it hurt too much to even think about trying to move my left hand or anything brave and heroic like that.

I was shaking all over, my guts felt like some joker had tied a big knot in them, and after a minute or so I realised that the warm, wet pool I was sitting in was my own piss. Really, you can't get lower than that and still be alive.

Just as well, then, that nothing came bothering me while I was in that state. If it had, there wasn't anything I could've done about it. I wouldn't have tried to fight or anything, I was too scared and sick and sorry for myself. No idea how long I stayed squatting there. Time's different in the dark, anyhow. I just sat and let it take its course. I think I may have dropped off to sleep, even.

But there came a time when I thought, The hell with this, I can't just stay here for ever. Then I got to thinking. The people who built these tunnels, the giants of old or whoever the fuck they were, they must've built them for a reason, and surely there was a good chance they built them with more than one entrance – in which case, even if I chose the wrong direction, surely it wasn't impossible I'd come out into the light again somewhere, eventually. And maybe there was a whole nest of Them down there, but maybe there was just the one, and I'd killed it, or at least hurt it so bad it wouldn't want to tangle with me any more. So I hadn't got a clue which way to go. So what? Think about it. The only stone-cold certainty was that if I stayed put where I was, bleeding into a pool of my own piss, I was definitely going to die. All the other choices I could make stood me in some chance of getting out. Really, I had nothing to lose, did I?

So I stood up. Not a good idea, because my knees folded up and I landed back on my bum in the pool of piss, and when I tried getting up again my feet slid in it, and that was just humiliating. So I crawled for a bit until I felt able to stand up straight, and after that I took it nice and slowly, counting twenty-five steps, then stopping to rest and listen and sniff.

The smells that had drowned everything else out back at the junction were starting to fade. I could make out blood, still, and sweat that wasn't my own. I went on further, and if anything the smells got stronger. After a bit I stopped and thought about it, and I reckoned it must mean I wasn't going back the way I'd come. Instead, I was following the way it had taken, running away from me.

I nearly turned round and went back, but I thought, No, screw that. If I go back, I'll only come to the junction again, and I don't suppose I've got all the time in the world for figuring it out by trial and error. Besides, I was so horribly tired, I couldn't face the thought of that long trek back. Press on, I told myself, and see what happens. It sounds stupid, making a choice like that basically out of laziness, but at the time it seemed a perfectly reasonable thing to do.

I'd have felt so much better if I'd still had the knife. Stupid, really, how one small thing, one possession, can mean so much when you haven't got it. After all, it's only a short, flat metal stick. If I'd been back at the Board offices, I could've gone and seen the stores clerk and explained how I'd lost my knife, and he'd have given me a new one, or maybe two or three if he happened to be in a good mood. He'd have thought nothing of it, and neither would I.

In the dark, though, I understood a really

important thing, about people, about the human race. In this world, I realised, there's two sorts of people. There's people with knives, and they survive; and there's people without, and they die. It's a pretty simple proposition, doesn't take a great deal of intelligence to figure out how it works, but there's nothing in the world that matters nearly as much as that one basic fact. And the bastard part of it is, you only figure it out when you've lost your knife and can't get another one.

But I kept going anyhow, because I had a feeling that if I stopped, I wouldn't be able to get started again, and that'd be it. I walked and I walked, until my knees ached and my back hurt and my feet were killing me. Don't ever let anybody kid you into believing you can't be bored stiff and scared stiff at the same time. It's a funny feeling, though. There's nothing on earth you'd like more than to sag down to the ground and lie there, but you know it's the one thing you daren't do. Oh, and I was thirsty as hell into the bargain, so bad I could hardly swallow, and the pain in my shoulder was getting worse all the time. I've felt better, and that's no lie.

55

I kept going, though, because I couldn't stop. By this point I was pretty light-headed, what with losing blood and getting bashed about so much, so I couldn't really trust what my ears and nose were telling me. Even so, I got the impression that there was something following me. Each time I stopped to listen, I couldn't hear anything, but when I started walking again, I was sure I could hear footsteps, just a fraction of a second later than my own.

At first I told myself it was just an echo, which was a safe enough guess in the tunnels. The thing was, though, it didn't sound like an echo. It was a different kind of footstep. It wasn't the grating of my heavy boot-soles on the smooth tiles, more like something soft. I thought of the pads on the soles of Their feet, and I began to feel seriously worried.

If I'd had the knife, I'd have tried to force a fight. I'd have stopped, or maybe even turned round and run back up the tunnel. With no knife and only one good arm, though, the last thing I wanted was any sort of fighting. So I tried to think it through. Couldn't be the bastard creature who'd bitten off my shoulder, I told myself. Of course I had no way of knowing exactly how much damage I'd done it, but it stood to reason it had to be in worse shape than me, so I found it hard to believe it'd want to fight it out with me. On the other hand, it now had my knife, and it knew I was empty-handed.

Perhaps it didn't know how badly it had hurt me. In that case, it could still think I was actively hunting it, and it could've made up its mind that the only way it was ever going to be rid of me was to kill me and get it over with. Or maybe it figured it was dying anyhow, so it might as well try and take me with it, to stop me hurting any more of its kind. Maybe it was just very, very angry, and didn't care. It hardly mattered. The only thing that counted for anything was that it was behind me, following me, taking great care not to be heard – stopping when I stopped – and that it was armed and I wasn't.

There's probably a very deep and significant point in there somewhere, about tables being turned, and the hunter hunted. If so, you're welcome to it. I was more concerned with trying to get out of those bloody tunnels. I knew I couldn't run, I just didn't have the strength. As far as I could judge, it was happy just matching me step for step, trailing along behind me like a tired dog after a long walk. By the sound of it, I was still a respectable distance ahead.

It was a bit like that proverb, holding a wolf by the ears – you can't hold it too long but you daren't let it go. Same with me, sort of. I couldn't go fast enough to get away from it, I couldn't stop dead in my tracks and risk facing it. All I could do was keep going, keep my distance, until it made up its mind whether it wanted to attack or not.

Stupid things go through your head at times like that. I tried to think about the woman it had killed, and the man upstairs in the house, but I couldn't get pictures of them in my mind. It was as though I'd only dreamed them, and you know how a dream just fades away the moment you wake up. I tried to think of other humans I'd seen killed by Them, but I couldn't. Instead, I kept seeing the one I'd killed earlier, crouching up on top of the junk-pile, watching me. That didn't help. I thought about predators, what it means to depend on killing other living things in order to keep alive yourself. That was what They did – I mean, I never heard of them being able to eat grass or plants or anything else but fresh meat – and of course it was what I did too, as a professional.

You know why I got into this line of work in the first place? Bloody stupid reason. My dad was a carpenter – very good one, too. He could saw a straight line lengthways through a three-inch-thick oak board without even scribing a line. All done by eye. Of course, everyone expected I'd join him in the workshop as soon as I was old enough. But I can't saw straight or plane or cut a mortice to save my life. He used to say, It's just practice, give the boy time and he'll get the hang of it. No chance. All I ever did was ruin good, expensive timber, until finally he got so mad at me he told me to get out of the workshop and stay out. After that, he talked to friends of his in other trades, but they all had sons and nephews of their own, they couldn't take on an apprentice.

Then one day one of Them came hunting round our way. It was only a young one, no more than three or four years old, and it hadn't got a clue – same as me, you see, no aptitude for the trade it was born into – but everybody down our street was scared shitless, because most of them had never seen one before, and those that had had lost family or friends to Them. And there I was, sixteen years old and fighting mad with the world.

I grabbed a chisel off the bench and went looking for the bastard thing, and it didn't take much finding. It was scrabbling away at someone's back door, like a dog wanting to come in out of the rain. It didn't hear me till I was right up close behind it, and before it could do anything I'd stuck the chisel into its neck, just behind the ear. It dropped like an apple off a tree. I jumped back, pulling the chisel out, but not quick enough to keep from getting blood squirted all over me. I didn't mind that. I remember standing over it watching it twitch – it curled up in a ball like a kitten sleeping, and its arms and legs flailed about for a bit, and then it sort of relaxed, like it had come home from a busy day.

Well, a minute or so later people started coming out of the houses, and when they saw what had happened they were cheering and hugging me, kicking it where it lay, you never saw such a fuss. I liked that, after all those years of being the useless kid in the neighbourhood, but it wasn't that I enjoyed most of all. What really pleased me was the feeling of having won.

Anyhow, not long after that I joined the Board, and it's been my trade ever since. Whatever pleasure there may have been in it wore off long ago, like it does with anything you do every day, for a living. It turned into just another day at work, something you forgot all about as soon as you got home and kicked your boots off. But thinking about it – like I was doing then, down the tunnel with my shoulder in shreds and no knife – I decided I must be some kind of predator too, by nature. Partly because I've got a gift for it, for want of a better word, but mostly because there wasn't anything else I could do to earn a living.

And I'm not going to kid you. I'm not going to pretend that there were days when I asked myself, Why am I doing this? Is it because I want to save people from Them, or is it because I like killing things? I never asked myself that, because I know the reason isn't really either of those two things. I hate it when I see what They do to people. You couldn't be human and not hate sights like that. But I don't fight to protect my fellow man. The people They kill are just strangers, after all, not anybody I know. I'm not a hero. I don't suppose I'd risk my life to save a stranger from a burning house. And I don't do it because I like to kill. Maybe that first time there was pleasure in it, but day in, day out, as a job – no. I do it because it's my living – my trade, same as Dad was a carpenter. Same as hunting us is Their trade.

Seems to me, there aren't any things in life that are always right or always wrong, not even killing Them, or any sort of killing. What makes it right or wrong is the side you happen to be on, whether it's you and your lot who are killing or getting killed.

CHAPTER FIVE

I SMELT IT A long way off. It's a smell you can't mistake for anything else, and it's always the same. It chokes you, no matter how used to it you are. The most you can ever do is ignore it. When you can't see or hear anything, and smell's your only link with the outside world, you can't even do that.

It was the smell of something that had been dead for a while – not too long, because it fades after about five days. My guess was, this was about three days old. I didn't like it, obviously, but I thought, Anything as dead as that isn't going to be able to hurt me. It's the live one behind me I need to worry about. So I kept on going.

I found it in the end. I walked into it. First thing I thought as the bones clattered under my feet was, Oh shit, the noise, but it was too late to worry about that, and besides, the bastard thing knew perfectly well where I was, it'd been tracking me for God knows how long.

In order to get round it without making any more of a row, I had to find it, and that meant groping about with my hands. Didn't take much searching, and I knew straight away what I'd found. The predator's larder, where it stashed the leftovers. I felt an arm, soft and wet, quite small – could've been a young woman, or a kid, I felt what I guessed was a shoulder, and a knee, and there was a head as well, I had no trouble identifying that. Long hair, which fitted in with it being a girl. In the dark, of course, I didn't have much to go on. But at least it made me angry.

I'm not sure why, though. Hadn't I just been thinking how it and I had so much in common – animals that kill to live, predators who need to take prey or else starve to death themselves? But that didn't seem to enter into it, somehow. I got angry because the bastard thing had gone up into the daylight, caught and killed one of us, dragged the dead meat back down into the dark and put it carefully away for later, when it fancied a snack. It had *won,* and somehow that meant I'd lost, it had beaten me, or us.

l couldn't help thinking that if I died down

there, I'd be another item of stores in its larder. I ran my fingers over the soft, pulpy skin of the dead face. I was buggered if I was going to let it have me too.

A betting man wouldn't have fancied my chances, though. My left arm was pretty much useless by that point – I could just about flex my fingers, but it hurt like hell – and I was getting very weak and woozy. I felt sore all over, and I was really, really tired. I wanted to keep going, but a little voice in my head told me it was just plain stupid, when all I had to do was sit down and soon it'd all be over. I told myself I'd just go a few more yards, get clear of the filthy stench, and then I'd sit down, for a minute or two.

I hadn't gone far when I heard a clatter, back behind me. It'd tripped over the dead body, same as I'd done. So it was still there, after all, and still following me. Somehow I'd hoped it might have packed it in and gone away, but I knew that wasn't likely. It had invested too much effort, pain and trouble in me to give up, and it had to know it was winning. And it had my knife.

The thought of that – my knife in its hand – made me go a bit faster, and I came to a bend in the tunnel, a sharp one. I felt my way round it with my fingertips, and suddenly I saw light.

It was as though someone had lit a fire inside my head. I shut my eyes, but the flare was still there, blotting and smudging everything into one great big white glow. To begin with I couldn't think what the hell it could be. Then I thought, God, I've made it, I've reached the end of the tunnel. I opened my eyes again (it hurt so much, but I made myself look) and slowly the flare got smaller, like it was soaking away, and I realised that what I was looking at was a single beam of light coming down from the roof of the tunnel.

I ran forward – it was incredible to be able to see, like I'd been blind all my life. I could see green stuff, moss or something of the kind, growing on the tunnel floor. I could see the colour of the tiles – they were a sort of greyish white, and green mould was growing up between them. It was all so beautiful, so much detail. I stopped and looked up at the place where the light was coming from, and I saw a shaft going straight up, twenty feet or more. At the top, so small I had trouble figuring out what it was, I saw a grating, like bars put up to keep an animal from escaping, or getting in.

I wanted to scream and yell, because for a few seconds I'd believed I was safe. But there was no way in hell I could've climbed up that shaft, not even with two good arms. It was enough to make you burst into tears. Like dying of thirst and seeing a lake twenty miles away, and knowing you'll never live to get there.

Even so, I was thinking, If I stay here in the light, it won't dare come near me. They're scared of the light, aren't they? I knew it wasn't true, of course. They come out into the light every day in order to feed. If I stayed there, sooner or later I'd pass out, and while I was asleep, it'd creep up and finish me off. Finding the light hadn't solved anything. All it had done was make my head hurt.

Thinking about it now, I suppose that was the moment when I came the closest to giving up. I had this stupid idea going round in my head: *Well, if you've got to die, you might as well die in the light.* Mostly, I guess, I didn't want to go back into the dark. In the little pool of light under that grating – I guess it was an old ventilation shaft, or something of the kind – I could see again. I could almost kid myself into believing that I was safe, that I was out, that I was home. A few steps down the tunnel would take me back into a world that hated me, where humans were never meant to be.

There's a lot of animals who live in the dark all the time – bats, mice, foxes. It's where they belong. My guess is that They belong there too. They don't need light like we do. What I had to get into my head was that the light wasn't the right place for me any more. I didn't belong there. They say that predators grow like the prey they hunt. I'd spent most of my life preying on predators, and look where it'd got me. Staying in the light, where normal people belong, would be the death of me. My only chance of staying alive lay in going back into the dark.

It was hard to do, though, but I managed it. I turned my back on the light, took one step and then another, and kept going, until the glow wasn't there any more, and it no longer mattered whether my eyes were open or shut.

The next smell was really familiar, but I couldn't think what it was. It seemed wrong somehow, out of place, like it shouldn't have been there. It belonged in another part of my life, and I couldn't understand what it was doing down there in the dark tunnels, with Them, and me.

Water. Suddenly I knew what it was. I could smell water.

Up here, where it's safe and I've got time to think clearly, I can figure it out easily enough. When the old giants built the tunnels, they must've come across an underground spring. Being giants, or whatever kind of incredibly wonderful super-beings they were, they knew how to build a tunnel so it was watertight. But that was a long time ago, and since the giants went away there hadn't been anybody to look after what they built, to patch it up and mend it. Gradually, the buried spring found a way through, as bricks and tiles crumbled and mortar came loose. Slowly, the lowest level of the tunnel started filling up with water, turning it into a kind of underground river.

I found it the way I'd found everything else, by blundering into it before I knew it was there. I heard the splash and felt the cold, clammy touch on my skin through my clothes. I smelt it, too – dirty, stagnant. It had gone bad, just like the dead girl I'd found earlier. Can water die? Well, if there's such a thing as dead water, that was what I walked into. To give you some idea, I'd never felt thirstier in my whole life, I'd have done anything for just enough water to wet my lips, but the thought of drinking that stuff never even crossed my mind.

I waded in, and the water level kept rising. I carried on going, and the water came in over my boots, then my knees, then my waist. Pretty soon I was having to push like mad just to force a way through. When it reached my neck, I stopped. I can't swim, see. If I went on any further, I'd drown.

I'd come to the end of the line.

I told myself, Well, this is it, then. Can't go any further or I drown. Stay here, and They'll get me. Mostly, I was bloody angry because I felt it just wasn't fair to be beaten by something crazy, like an underground river. Whoever it was who was playing these games with me, as far as I was concerned he was cheating.

So there I was. Wet through, stinking of filthy water, with one useless arm, no knife, dead tired. I couldn't go any further down the tunnel, so the only way out was back the way

I'd come, all that distance I'd dragged myself along. No more choices.

One good thing. It forced me to decide. Running away wasn't going to solve anything. Sooner or later, I was going to have to turn and face the bastard thing, and I was going to have to kill it, with my bare hands.

I sat down with my back to the wall, and I tried to think. What did I have? I still had my human brain. I said to myself, Why's it right that, in the end, we're going to win against those bastards and wipe Them off the face of the earth? What gives us that right? What makes us better? They're as strong as us, They're better than us at night, in the dark. They can jump further. They don't need weapons, They've got teeth and claws. What makes us better, and so gives us the right to win, is that we're smarter than they are. Life's a contest. You only come out on top if you deserve to win. If I wanted to beat the bastard thing and go on living, I had to do something to deserve the victory.

It was hard work, thinking, in the state I was in. My mind didn't want to seem to grip, like cartwheels on an icy road. It's like I was clawing

71

at a tiny gap, trying to prise it open with my fingernails, but it was too tight, too stiff. I thought—

I thought, How can I beat this thing?

I thought, Down here, it's got all the advantages. Even my knife. Down here, everything plays to its strengths – darkness, the fact that it's on its home ground.

I thought, If it hasn't got any weaknesses I can use, I guess I'd better make use of its strengths.

I thought, I bet there's one thing we've got in common, that bastard thing and me.

I thought of an idea.

It wasn't much of an idea, God knows. In fact, it was pretty pathetic, any way you chose to look at it. Really, you'd have to be pretty stupid to fall for it. In which case, I'd have to bet my life on my enemy being pretty stupid, at least compared to me. And that struck me as a pretty good way of deciding things, because if it was dumb enough to fall for the trick, then it didn't deserve to win. If it cottoned on and my stupid plan didn't work, then I didn't deserve to beat it and stay alive.

Oh well, I thought. Then I reached forward

and started untying my bootlaces.

Stage one of my stupid plan was easy. I got up and walked back down the tunnel, away from the underground river. I wasn't deliberately trying to make a noise, just walking. Having my bootlaces undone didn't help. My boots were too big for me – I got them from my uncle when he died, and he had big feet – and without the laces to keep them tight, my feet slopped about in them, which made it hard to walk normally.

I counted thirty paces under my breath, then stopped. That was what I'd been doing all along, so the bastard thing following me wouldn't have noticed anything out of the ordinary. I did the usual routine – stop, listen, sniff. Then I counted up to fifty and turned back, heading toward the underground river.

The idea was, make it think I was in two minds about what to do next. I wanted it to think I'd found the river, turned back, gone a little way, changed my mind, gone back again. The tricky part now was judging the distance exactly. Thirty paces, but what's a pace? It's the distance you travel in one stride, assuming your stride's always the same length. But I was cutting it fine. A few inches out, and I'd be screwed.

The real bugger was the sloppy boots. I couldn't just switch my mind off and trust myself to measure out thirty identical paces, because without the laces done up my boots felt strange, so I couldn't rely on instinct. I just had to do the best I could, and hope.

Thirty paces back again. Stop, for the listening-and-sniffling ritual. This time, though, while I was doing all that, I was bending down and taking my boots off. I couldn't afford to make even the slightest sound, and of course I was doing it all one-handed, which didn't help. It didn't matter whether the bastard thing figured out what I was doing or not. All it'd take would be for it to realise I was doing something different, and that'd put it on its guard. I managed it, though. I stood there with my boots in my one good hand, swung my arm back, and threw them as far as I could make them go.

They landed in the water with a splash. I yelled out, like I'd just fallen in the water myself.

The next bit had to be real quick and smooth. I pulled off my coat – one-handed again, it's really not easy taking a coat off with just one hand – and flattened myself against the wall, with my left leg stuck out in front of me. Really, I needed to make more splashing noises, but I couldn't think of any way of doing that, so I did more yelling and swearing. Had to make it sound like I was in trouble in the water. It was pretty bloody unconvincing, and I remember thinking, this is never going to work, I'm screwed. Then I heard what I'd been hoping I'd hear. Footsteps, running.

I held my breath.

Up they came, the footsteps. To get the timing right, I tried thinking it through as though I was the bastard thing, put myself into its tiny mind. I've heard the splash, which tells me my enemy's fallen in the water. I've heard it howling and yelling. It wouldn't do that unless it was in trouble. Maybe it can't swim and it's drowning. Now's my chance. I start running. I've got to get there while it's weak so I can finish it off safely. Hurry. I run. I can hear my own footsteps slapping on the tiles. I live down here in these tunnels, so I know exactly how far it is to the water. This is my one chance to finish it and survive. Hurry—

I heard it coming, the bastard thing, and I

braced myself, hoping I'd stuck my leg out in the right place. It all depended, see, on whether I'd counted out the thirty paces right. If I had, I was standing right at the water's edge, so when the bastard thing came running up and tripped over my leg, it'd go face-down in the water, where I wanted it to be. If not – well, that water was my only weapon. If I'd got it wrong and it fell on the dry tiles, I didn't reckon my chances much.

I could feel it coming. As it ran, it pushed its way through the air, and I could feel the slight breeze. I yelled one more time, to reassure it and give it a definite fix on my position. I felt it, a ghastly jarring thump against my shin. I heard a splash, and drops of water hit me in the face. If I got the next bit wrong, I might as well forget it.

Holding my coat out in front of me, I made myself fall forward, right on top of it. As I landed – its head was round and hard, and it knocked all the breath out of me – I reached out with my good arm and hugged at it, wrapping the coat round it. Simple enough idea. Use the coat like a net, get a grip on it and hold it tight. Hold its face down in the water and drown it.

Like I said at the start, a pretty stupid plan, but the best I could do in the circumstances.

I wasn't expecting it to wriggle so much or be *so* damned strong. It was all elbows and knees and claws – but I had the coat, to keep from getting scratched and ripped up. My guess is, it was stronger than me, but I was heavier, and that was all that counted. I didn't have to outfight it or beat it at wrestling. I just had to make it breathe in water. It always helps if you keep it simple, I generally find.

It screamed. I wasn't expecting that, either. The noise scared me, almost enough to make me let go. Instead, it made me grip tighter. Even then, with my life in the balance, I couldn't help thinking, This is a bloody odd way to kill something, hugging it to death in six inches of water. It screamed again, and this time it was a horrible, comical sort of noise, half screaming and half gurgling. Wonderful, I thought, I've got its head in the water, won't be long now, just so long as I don't let go—

It screamed and gurgled again, and I put all my last few scraps of strength into my arm and my shoulder, pushing past the pain. It screamed and gurgled, this time more gurgle

77

than scream. I was so happy, I wanted to laugh.
So nearly there—

'Please,' it said. 'Please.'

CHAPTER SIX

THERE ARE MOMENTS WHEN everything changes. It's like you've been asleep and you wake up, and you can't remember where you are or how you got there. It's like you've just been let in on a secret that everybody else knows but you. It's like finding out that the man you've called Dad all your life isn't your real father.

I never knew they could talk.

I stopped trying to hold its head in the water. Suddenly, killing it stopped being the most important thing in the world. In fact, I really didn't want to touch it at all. The moment I let it go, of course, I knew I'd done something really stupid. It could twist round and stab me or bite me and there'd be nothing I could do about it. But it hardly moved. I could hear it breathing, great big desperate gulps of air.

'Give me back my knife,' I said.

It was just the first thing that came into my

head, now that I could talk to it. I heard something clatter on the tiles. As easy at that, apparently. I reached down, scrabbled about in the water, and my fingertips brushed against the staghorn handle. I grabbed it and snatched it away, like a kid with a toy he doesn't want the other kids to take off him.

Getting the knife back was like sunlight and heat and food when you're hungry and water when you're dry. It was almost as if I could hear the knife screaming inside my head, Go on, do it, finish it, now. But I couldn't.

'You can talk, then,' I said.

'Yes. So can you.'

It was the strangest-sounding voice you ever heard. I mean, when you meet someone for the first time, isn't one of the most important things the sound of their voice? It tells you so much. Where's he from, is he rich or poor, is he one of us or one of them? As soon as someone opens their mouth, you know pretty much everything worth knowing about him. But that thing's voice – oh, that was something else entirely. I could understand it, no problem. I mean, I've had more trouble understanding upcountry people. But it was – I don't know, I can't describe it. It was a perfectly ordinary voice, but no way you'd mistake it for human. It was a voice shaped by a totally different design of tongue and mouth. It was what animals would sound like, if they could talk.

'Well,' it said, 'are you going to kill me?'

'Stay there,' I said. 'Don't bloody move.'

'Are you going to kill me?'

Thirty seconds earlier, that'd have been a bloody stupid question. 'You've been trying to kill me,' I said. 'Why the hell shouldn't I?'

It didn't reply to that. I was still feeling stunned. How come, I thought, how come after all these years we never knew they could talk? 'Get up,' I said.

'I don't think I can,' it replied.

'Get up, or I'll fucking kill you.'

'Oh, in that case.' It made a sort of grunting noise, just like one of us would if we were badly hurt. I put the knife into the fingers of my buggered hand and closed them around the grip, then reached out and groped about until I felt its fur. 'Back up the tunnel,' I said. 'I want to look at you in the light.'

'Why?'

'Don't argue.'

81

I closed my fingers in its fur. Somehow I knew it wasn't going to attack me now. It was too weak, something like that. I let it come round me. I was banking on it not knowing I only had one good arm. It was all wet, of course, where it'd been in the water. I held on to its fur like a horseman holding reins, and I let it lead me up the tunnel. It seemed a very long way to the light, but we got there.

This time, the light still hurt but it didn't freak me out entirely, like it had before. I remember I was staring in front of me as we got closer to it, and gradually I began to make out the shape of its head, turning from a vague grey shape into something I could recognise. It was a bit like watching a sunrise, the way that you begin to be able to see more and more detail, until each blade of grass stands out sharp and clear. I saw the shape of its ears, the collar of the heavy padded jacket it had on, finally the grain of the hairs of its fur.

'Stop there,' I said.

It stopped and kept still.

The first thing I needed to see was the wounds I'd made where I'd stabbed it. Not hard to find. There were big dark patches all round them, where the blood had soaked out into the jacket and caked on the fur of its leg. There were little dark red crystals of dried blood caught in the hairs, like dewdrops in the long grass.

'Turn round,' I said.

It was one hell of a shock, seeing its face. I'm not sure you could even call it a face. I mean, they don't have noses and mouths like we do, they look more like cats or pigs than people, and their eyes are a different shape, with a black slash in the middle instead of a round pupil. I looked at it, and all I could see was a savage animal that killed people. But savage animals can't talk.

'So?' it said. 'Have you decided yet?'

I let go of its fur and took a step back. 'How the hell did you learn to talk?' I said. 'Can you all do it, or are you different from the others?'

'We learn the same way you do,' it replied, 'from our parents. We talk to each other all the time. We just don't talk to you.'

I couldn't think of the right words for any of the questions I wanted to ask. So I just said, 'Why not?'

It blinked. 'What would be the point?'

That just made me mad, 'If we talked to each

other, maybe we wouldn't have to kill each other all the time.'

'We hunt you,' it said. 'You hunt us. What difference would talking make?'

'But you don't have to hunt us,' I said, 'and then we wouldn't hunt you.'

It blinked again. 'That's stupid,' it said. 'We need to eat, same as you.' It shivered, right down from its head to its feet. I couldn't tell if that was because it was hurting, or just a gesture, like shrugging your shoulders. 'We don't talk, because we have nothing to say to each other. Isn't that obvious?'

I wanted to ask. Where did you come from, why did you come here, what are you, who are you? I wanted to ask how badly it was hurt – was it dying, or would it recover – because clearly its body was different from mine, I didn't know how badly it was damaged. I wanted to ask why they never killed cows or sheep, only people. I wanted to ask if there could be peace, because surely, if you can talk to someone, you don't have to fight any more. I wanted to be the man who ended the war and changed the world.

'Kneel down,' I said.

It looked at me, and its ears went back, the way a horse's ears go back when it thinks there's danger. I shifted the knife back into my right hand.

'You're badly hurt,' it said. 'Your shoulder. I didn't know I'd done so much damage.'

'Kneel down,' repeated.

Its eyes widened a bit, and it knelt down, 'What are you going to do?' it asked.

'I'm not sure,' I lied.

You see, there's a time and a place for everything. I remember when I was a kid, and for some reason times were really hard. My dad hadn't got any work coming in, and there was never enough to eat. But a mile or so down the road there was an old woman who kept geese. Miserable old bitch she was, always threw stones at us kids if she saw us round her place.

Well, one day I was down there, just mucking about, and I saw one of her big fat geese waddling up the road. It must've got out somehow. Maybe she'd left a gate open, or the fox had got in and scared them all stupid, and this one had flown out of the yard, I don't know. But there it was – huge great thing, all

85

muddy brown and grey – and I suddenly thought, we could have that for dinner.

I looked round, and there was a nice round stone, just the right size to slip in my hand, so I picked it up and chucked it at this goose, and as luck would have it I got it right in the head. It went down and started flapping about like crazy. I nearly panicked and ran for it, but thought, Well, I've bashed the stupid thing's brains in, if I leave it now it'd be such a waste. I jumped up, grabbed the goose round the neck and tried to throttle it. But it's not as easy as it looks, necking a goose. I yanked and twisted and pulled, but the bugger wouldn't die, it just thrashed and honked and struggled, so I pulled harder and harder, until suddenly its head just came off in my hand.

I let go of it – I could see the windpipe sticking out of its neck – and I wanted to throw up, but somehow that made me even more determined to get it home and cooked. So I jumped up again, slung it over my shoulder and ran for it. But that bloody goose, I don't know what it must've weighed, but I was only little. I lugged it on my back until my neck hurt so much I couldn't stand it any more. I wrapped my arms round it and tried carrying it that way, but that was worse. I even dragged it along by its feet for a bit. But the time came when I was so tired out I couldn't go another step, not even crawling on my hands and knees.

It was quite simple. The goose was too big for me. I'd have to dump it. So I looked at it, and a right old mess it was by then – all covered in blood and dust, feathers all tangled and busted up where I'd been dragging it. It looked comic and disgusting and stupid, and I hated it for being all spoilt. I hated the thought that I'd killed it and worn myself out getting it that far, and now it would all go to waste. But I was too tired. I was too small to do the job I'd set myself. It just wasn't possible. So I dragged it under a hedge and left it, and went home.

It was that same feeling, I suppose. There was this big thing I could do. That I could've done, rather, if I hadn't been tired out and all carved up where it'd bitten me. Which is just another way of saying, if I'd been big enough to get the job done, I could've talked to it, reasoned with it, explained things. I could've found out the things about Them that we don't know, and told it about us. And then, maybe—

But God help me, I was so tired, and my arm hurt, and I was scared, and it was so much easier the other way.

'How many more of you are there down here?' I asked.

'Just one,' it said. 'It's just me and my son.'

'The one who came with you to the village today?'

'Yes.' It looked up at me. 'What happened to him? Do you know?'

I looked at it. 'No,' I said. I could tell it knew I was lying. But it'd told me what I needed to know. There weren't any more of them down there. I believed what it told me. Somehow, I don't think They can tell lies, like we can. 'Keep still,' I said.

I went round behind it, and you know what? It didn't move, not at all. When I was in position, I leaned forward against the back of its neck, and stabbed the knife into the side of its head, right through the bare patch of skin directly under its ear. It jerked away from me, twisting the knife out of my hand, and fell forward. I jumped back. It stretched right out, then folded up. I watched it shiver a couple of times, and then it made a sort of very soft, gentle sighing noise, and that was that.

I counted up to twenty before pulling out the knife, just in case, but there wasn't any need.

I really wanted to sit down and rest, but I couldn't stick the thought of looking at it any more, so I set off walking, back into the dark. I wasn't thinking about what I was doing or where I needed to go. I was too busy not thinking, if you see what I'm getting at. Call it fool's luck if you like, but I took all the right turnings this time. How long it took me I can't say, but eventually I wandered out of the tunnel back into the light.

Once I was out, I dropped down on the ground and lay there for a bit, just staring up at the sky. But it was getting dark, and you don't want to be outside at night anywhere They might be prowling around. I got up and headed back to the village. First door I came to, I bashed on it and kicked and yelled till some old woman opened it. She told me to piss off. I think I may have threatened to cut her head off if she didn't let me in, I can't remember too clearly.

Next morning, the village people came to see me. They told me they thought I was dead, and I was a hero, and was there anything they could do for me? I said yes, I needed to get the body of the one I'd killed back out of the tunnel, because if I didn't have a body to show to the Board I wouldn't get paid. I explained that it'd be perfectly safe, because there were just the two of them down there and I'd killed them both. I said I'd have gone myself, only I was too badly chewed up. They said they were very sorry about my arm and they'd send for the doctor, but they weren't going down any tunnels, not for anybody. Not their job, they said. That's what we pay people like you for.

People like me, they said. Fair comment.

I've quit the trade now, of course. No choice. I'm getting some feeling back in the arm, but I'll never be able to work again. For a long time, I wanted to tell someone about what I'd found out the fact that They can talk, but in the end I thought, The hell with it. It ought to make a difference, of course, in an ideal world. But the world's not ideal, is it? No way. How could it be, when it's got things like Them, and people like me?